About the author

William Taylor was born long ago, near the sleepy village of Manchester, in the land of England.

He was born in the traditional manner – naked in a room full of strangers. Before long, he was educated – and very quickly learned the basics of tying both shoelaces and a tie.

He became a man and took himself a wife (he didn't steal one, he got married). Now he likes to write down his silly thoughts and musings, occasionally wondering what happened to the boy he once was…

The Bee Polisher

William B Taylor

The Bee Polisher

Illustrated by Helen Gerrard

Pegasus

A CIP catalogue record for this title is
available from the British Library

ISBN: 978 1 910903 23 0

Pegasus is an imprint of
Pegasus Elliot MacKenzie Publishers Ltd.
www.pegasuspublishers.com

First Published in 2019

Pegasus
Sheraton House Castle Park
Cambridge CB3 0AX England

Printed & Bound in Great Britain

Dedication

In fond memory of Wizardmarra – a.k.a. Alan Whittaker.

Acknowledgements

The author would like to thank his wife, Helen Gerrard.

Thanks to the Taylor and Gerrard families.

A special thank you to Rae Leeson for all his hard work and support – he knows about things.

The Kingdom of Bumblonia was a beautiful land whose farms produced the plumpest vegetables and the sweetest fruit. Each and every spring the land awoke, and was transformed by the vibrant colours of countless wild flowers, in all sorts of varieties.

The ruler of Bumblonia, King Garold, lived in The Royal Twill, a castle high up on a hill from where he could see the beauty of the unspoiled land and breathe the fresh, clean air. He was a humble and kindly king, who loved the land and his people, and they loved him too. There were many festivals and celebrations to enjoy and everyone was truly happy and content.

The villagers of Bumblonia were friendly, hard-working folk. Mainly farmers, they worked the land to produce enough food to keep them more than satisfied. Nobody went hungry and nobody was ever grumpy (except for the odd occasion when a young farmhand might have celebrated a little too hard the night before, with perhaps a little too much scrumpy, which was perhaps a little too tasty). These occasional feelings never lasted long because local remedies from fresh herbs, plenty of fresh air and plenty more fresh, clean water would soon do the trick and have them on their feet again.

Sadly, the day came when King Garold, after many years of ruling, died of very, very old age. The villagers all came together to speak of their love for King Garold and to celebrate his reign and his good long life. The heir to the throne, Prince Barold, had long since decided he didn't want to be a ruler, instead choosing to dedicate his life to the hunting and studying of mushrooms. Barold had left with his father's blessing and love, and strangely hadn't been seen since, although rumours of a crazy, dancing man in the forest seemed to circulate every autumn since the prince had left.

The next in line to the throne of Bumblonia was the old King's niece, Malicia, who had been brought up in the neighbouring Kingdom of Shmogg. She had spent most of her years in Shmogg painting her face and trying on expensive dresses. Malicia had never visited the countryside before; she believed it to be a dirty place, full of uneducated and uncivilised people.

She preferred to stay in the city, where the smoke from the chimneys meant that educated men were industriously creating lavish luxuries for those that could afford them, and where people were so civilised, they wouldn't tell you to your face if they had a problem with you; they would very respectfully spread rumours about you amongst your friends and maybe take any left over, bottled-up frustrations out on their servants.

Upon hearing the news of her uncle's death, Malicia was unmoved. She had met King Garold only the once when she was a child. He had actually smiled at her. Nobody had ever smiled at her before, especially a grown-up. She had seen grown-ups grin on occasion, usually whilst cackling and rubbing their hands together. The smile had confused her and Malicia did not like being confused. She knew what she was used to and she was used to what she knew, and she didn't want or need anything else, except perhaps another expensive dress or two.

Upon hearing she was duty-bound to travel to Bumblonia, to live there and rule over a rabble of dirty, uncivilised farmers, Malicia was furious.

"I shan't go!" she shrieked. "It's dirty and horrid and you can't make me!" She stamped her foot hard on the floor. Realising she had missed her handmaiden's foot, Malicia aimed a bit to the right and stamped her foot again, harder.

Her father, Lord Shmuck, Duke of Shmogg and surrounding areas, wiped his fat, sweaty forehead with an expensive, initialed silk handkerchief.

"But you must go, Malicia, darling," he said. "It's expected, it's your duty."

"Why it is my duty?" barked Malicia.

"If you don't do your duty, all our privileges would be taken from us. We'd be poor!" Lord Shmuck paused, then added, "You would be a queen…"

Malicia considered the idea of being poor. She didn't understand poor people and the thought of being one of them did not appeal to her at all.

"Well, I shall need guards, and a new wardrobe. What do they wear in Bumblonia?"

"I believe they wear sensible jumpers, strong trousers and something called Wellington boots." Replied Lord Shmuck, relieved that Malicia seemed to be coming around to the idea.

"In that case, I want the most beautiful sensible jumper ever made, with gold and jewels all over."

"As you wish, darling." Sighed Lord Shmuck.

"And the finest, strongest trousers that will surely dazzle my lowly subjects," continued Malicia, "made from the finest silks from across the seas."

"It shall be seen to, sweet child."

"And my Wellington boots will be made by the finest craftsmen in the world."

"Your wish…"

"Out of glass, like in the fairy stories."

"… is my command."

Lord Shmuck wiped his brow again.

The day of the coronation arrived. The great hall in The Royal Twill had been decorated with beautiful flowers and the tables has been laid with bowls of sweet, succulent fruit. The guests, all nobles and wealthy merchants, waited in anticipation of the forthcoming ceremony.

Princess Malicia entered to a fanfare of trumpets, escorted by her guard and looking resplendent in the most elaborate sensible jumper anybody had ever seen. Her strong, silk trousers flowed down her legs and were a wonder to behold. On her feet, a pair of beautiful glass Wellington boots sparkled like no pair of Wellington boots had ever sparkled before.

She was relieved she hadn't bothered to invite any of

the local farmers. They would not have known how to properly behave in such a regal environment and anyway, they would probably just have made the place look a bit scruffy. An archbishop had needed to be imported into the kingdom to conduct the coronation. There were no archbishops in Bumblonia as they had never felt they needed one. He stood by the throne in his long robes and a massive pointy hat.

Princess Malicia proceeded down the aisle, her guests grinning appropriately as she passed by them. At the altar, she knelt, as she had been taught to. The archbishop spoke in a voice loud enough for all there to hear.

"Princess Malicia, as true heir to the throne of the Kingdom of Bumblonia, I crown you..." pause for effect, "Queen Malicia of Bumblonia, Ruler of the valley and protector of all life therein."

He picked up a large, jewel encrusted, gold crown (this had to be specially made for the occasion as the previous kings and queens of Bumblonia had never bothered with crowns of gold before; they were considered impractical as they are heavy and take ages to polish. At festivals and celebrations, a simple wreath made form whatever flora was in season at the time was considered a fine enough crown for any occasion). The archbishop's arms shook with the sheer effort of holding it. He placed the crown on the new queen's head with a sigh of relief.

"Arise, Queen Malicia of Bumblonia, Ruler of the valley and protector of all life therein."

The new queen stood to yet another fanfare of trumpets, the huge gleaming crown perched precariously on her head. The blare from the trumpets drowned out the sound of a quiet buzzing noise coming from the vicinity of the throne.

"Your Majesty," announced the archbishop. "The throne of the Kingdom of Bumblonia is yours!"

She walked majestically towards the throne, turned towards her grinning audience and sat down.

"Aaaargh!" Queen Malicia leapt, screaming, several feet into the air, clutching the seat of her strong silk trousers.

"Aaaargh! Assassins! Murder! Aaaargh! Guards, guards!"

The queen's guards raced towards the throne. There was nobody there. "Erm, there's nobody there, Your Majesty." Said the captain.

"How dare you!" Screamed the queen. "I have been attacked! I have been assaulted and stabbed! Find the villain and bring him to me right now!"

The guards began searching the great hall. One guard, searching near the throne, stopped. Looking at the floor, he knelt for a better look.

"Captain, I think I've found something." He called.

The captain walked across and also knelt. He craned his neck and scratched his head.

"Hmm," he said. "What have we got here then?" The other guards began to gather round.

"What's that?" Asked one.

"I don't know," replied another.

"I've never seen nothing like that back in Shmogg before." Came another voice from within the huddle of guards.

"Could be some sort of poison dart, maybe?" ventured

another. The queen was getting impatient.

"Captain!" She demanded. "Bring it to me at once!"

The captain picked up the object of interest gingerly. He approached the queen, holding it on the palm of his outstretched hand. The queen studied it closely. It was very small, with yellow and black stripes.

"What is it Captain? And what is it doing on my throne?"

"I, erm… I don't know, Your Majesty." Replied the captain nervously. It was never good to admit to not knowing something around posh and high society circles.

"Archbishop! You've read a book! Tell me what this thing is." The archbishop stroked his beard and frowned.

"It's nothing I've seen or heard of before, and I've read a book…" he looked closer and shook his head. After a moment, he turned to the queen.

"As we all know," he spoke in a voice loud enough for all there to hear. "I have indeed read a book. Not just any book, it was a good book. Not just any good book but the Good Book. I know that because it says it loud and clear itself."

The congregation in the great hall waited expectantly to hear what further educated wisdom the archbishop might impart.

"This thing... this creature... is NOT in the Good Book! Do you know what that means?" he asked theatrically.

Murmurs from everybody in the hall seemed to indicate that they did not know what that meant.

"It means..." the archbishop paused for effect. "It means if it is not in The Good Book, it must be bad!"

Gasps from all around the hall indicated to the archbishop that he had everyone's full and undivided attention.

"It therefore stands to reason," he continued, "that this offending creature, a beast not of the good book," - another pause for effect - "must be..." - the hall was so quiet you could hear a pin drop - "a demon!"

Queen Malicia screamed as the hall descended into shouts of panic and general chaos. Chairs were toppled and tables were turned over, spilling the fruit across the floor which was subsequently squashed underfoot on the tiles in the mayhem. Eventually, the queen steeled herself and ordered the crowd to be silent. They obeyed.

"I am the Queen of Bumblonia, Ruler of the valley and protector of all life therein." She proclaimed. "I shall not allow demons in my kingdom." Malicia turned to the captain of the guard.

"As your queen, my first decree is that you take the guards and round up all these demons that are befouling the kingdom and lock them up in the dungeon."

"As you wish, Your Majesty," said the Captain, with a

bow. "Guards! You heard Her Majesty! On the double, left, right, left, right…"

The guards marched out of the castle, leaving Queen Malicia seething with rage, surrounded by her terrified guests and squashed fruit.

Old Fred the farmer kept a small farm near the tiny village of Coombe. It sat at the bottom of the valley, at the foot of the mountains, by a clear stream, teeming with fish. He had grown prize-winning vegetables and had been champion three years running at Bumblonia's annual fruit and vegetable festival. His small orchard produced apples, pears and plums so juicy and sweet they had been a favourite of the old King Garold.

The lane leading down towards Hunningbie Farm was lined with wild flowers. The farmhouse was a cosy, thatched cottage with a rickety gate and a modest farmyard with a few chickens, geese and some ducks. There was also a barn which housed Old Fred's plough and his beloved cow, Milky Joe. In the orchard, Old Fred kept a few beehives, just enough to provide honey for himself, and maybe a pot or two extra he could give to friends on special occasions.

Soon news about the events at The Royal Twill

reached Coombe. Old Fred ran a small market stall in the village square every Monday and Thursday. This particular Thursday, as he rolled his cart of fresh fruit and vegetables into the village square, he noticed the atmosphere was different than usual. Groups of traders that would ordinarily be setting up shop and getting ready for an honest day's trading were instead crowding in little groups, chattering excitedly amongst themselves. In one of the groups, Old Fred spotted Young Bill, the butcher's boy.

"How do, Young Bill." Said Old Fred, approaching the group.

"Hello, Old Fred," replied Young Bill. "Have you heard? There's been a right kerfuffle up 'Twill."

"Has there now?" asked Old Fred. "They'll soon settle down, they may be city folk but they'll get to grips with the countryside before long."

"I don't know about that, Old Fred," said Frankie, the fishmonger. "I've heard tell the new queen's a bit mad."

"Oh, how so?" asked Old Fred.

"Well, you know Lean Larry, the landlord?"

"Yes."

"Well, he told me that Big Barry told him that the queen thinks there's demons in Bumblonia."

"Big Barry the blacksmith or Big Barry the barrow boy?" asked Old Fred.

"Big Barry the barrow boy." Replied Frankie.

"Did they give her the especially strong special scrumpy at the castle by accident?" asked Old Fred.

"No," said Frankie. "They got all them posh wines from over the sea, they didn't want our scrumpy."

"That'll be that then," said Old Fred. "Foreign wine, doesn't do no good to nobody, that stuff."

"It's not just that!" said Young Billy the butcher's boy excitedly. "There's talk of soldiers going around rounding up all the bees and locking them up!"

"Hmm," said Old Fred. "No good will come of that…"

Later that evening, back on Hunningbie Farm, Old Fred sat in the farmyard on an upturned pail, smoking his pipe. He was deep in thought.

"I don't know, Milky Joe. There's bad times afoot when folk go around locking up bees."

Milky Joe looked at Old Fred through the top of the barn door. "Moo."

"I mean, what does she want all them bees for anyway?"

"Moo."

"Do they eat bees in the city or something?"

No answer. Feeling he might be upsetting Milky Joe with his melancholy, Old Fred decided he would take a walk around the orchard for a while to clear his head.

The evening air was cool, with a slight breeze that wafted the smoke from his pipe towards the end of the orchard where Fred kept his beehives. He followed the smoke until he reached the hives. Most of his bees had finished their work for the day; only a few were left, buzzing lazily around as if they had the same sense of some impending unknown that Old Fred felt.

He sat down beneath an apple tree, pondering the gravity of the situation. "Well bees, my lovelies." Old Fred often talked to the bees when he was on his own. He didn't for a moment believe they understood him when he rambled on about things like what had maybe happened that day, who he had met or what he had chatted about with the village folk, but it somehow seemed to make him feel better.

"What a day," Old Fred mused. "Who would've thought it could come to this?"

He took a pull on his pipe, trying to make some sense of the day's events. He blew the smoke out slowly, watching the curls and rings drift gently past the beehives before drifting up to possibly join the clouds at the mountain tops.

"Yesterday, everything was normal," Old Fred went on. "The only news of any sort was hearing about how one of Shaggy Sean's lambs had gone missing, only to be discovered having wandered off out of sight behind a tree. Today it's mad queens, demons and gangs of soldiers arresting bees."

Old Fred took another pull on his pipe. He couldn't bear the idea of soldiers barging in and taking his cherished bees away.

"How in the world am I going to be able to hide all my bees?" He spoke aloud to himself, and his bees.

"I'll show you how." Said a voice.

The Royal Twill bustled with activity as the guards went about their important royal task. Special dungeons had had to be built for the bee prisoners, not only because bees are a lot smaller than the average guest at the average majesty's pleasure, but because there had never before been the need for dungeons in the kingdom. There were secure rooms in some of the watchmen's houses, but these were only ever used for the occasional drunken farmer who had temporarily either forgotten where they lived or forgotten how to physically get home.

Queen Malicia stood on the balcony overseeing the movements of her guards as they marched out of the castle in their shining armour, proud and determined to be carrying out their royal orders. She also watched as they returned with their captives, many a soldier worse for wear having been stung whilst out on bee hunting manoeuvres. The captain of the guard stood by her side as they discussed how the campaign was coming along.

"We've cleared nearly half the Kingdom now, Your Majesty. The troops are doing their bravest best, but the enemy is cunning, quick and dangerous. I worry the men may soon start losing their morale; the little blighters have a nasty sting and our stocks of ointment are getting worryingly low."

The Queen paced back and forth.

"The devils may be cunning, but we must be smarter than them, Captain."

"The villagers are not too happy about it either. They're not resisting yet but there's a growing feeling of unrest across the land. I fear there could be an uprising if this drags on for too long."

"Why should the peasants want these… these bees, or

whatever they call the horrible little things, around anyway? They are dangerous, just look what they have done to your men already."

The Captain was embarrassed for his men. They had assumed the job would be easy, the creatures were a lot smaller than his soldiers, and they had spears and swords. He wondered how far the patience of the Queen could be stretched before it would snap, perhaps horridly, and with consequences he might wish to avoid.

"I don't know, Ma'am," he replied. "They don't seem to mind them. Some of them even keep them on their land. It makes no sense."

"Of course it makes sense, Captain!" barked the Queen. "It makes perfect sense, it is the demon's trickery. They have been enchanted, they are bewitched! We need to wake them up, open their eyes and show them the evil spell that they are under right now. We need a campaign to win their hearts and minds. We need them to want to get rid of the bees for their own well-being."

"Brilliant, Your Majesty!" The captain was impressed by Queen Malicia's plan. "That might just work…"

Old Fred looked around the orchard to see who had spoken. He often heard voices but usually they were either other people near him or his own voice talking to himself. He did not recognise this voice. It was soft and quiet, but not weak. At first, he couldn't see anybody there but as he turned back to face the beehives, he noticed a cloaked figure in the dusk.

The first thing Old Fred noticed was the height of the fellow; he couldn't be more than a foot tall, which was rather short for people in these parts. The strange little man approached and as he got nearer to Fred, he could see he looked very old. He walked with a stick, although he did not seem to have a limp and did not seem to be very frail. Old Fred noticed that the bees had started humming in their hives.

"Hello there," said Old Fred. "Can I help you?"

"Not unless you're any good at foot rubs, my feet hurt." Replied the stranger.

"Sorry to hear that, friend. I don't know anything about foot rubbing but you're welcome to sit and rest your feet here for a while and share my pipe. I've got some scrumpy here somewhere, if you'd care for a drop?" Old Fred was generous to a fault; he reasoned if you can't be kind to a stranger, why should a stranger be nice to you? He produced a flask from his pocket and offered it to the little man.

"Thank you, Old Fred, you're very kind." The stranger took the flask.

"No prob… erm, how do you know my name?" asked Old Fred, not massively surprised. Everybody in Coombe knew Old Fred the farmer, his produce kept most of them fed. Many more people throughout the Kingdom would have heard of his prize-winning marrows and pumpkins. Even good old King Garold had been partial to Old Fred's juicy fruit and vegetables.

"I know you, Old Fred. I know you grow the best crops in the land."

"Why, thank you." Said Old Fred.

"You keep the people fed with good, healthy food and you are greatly respected." Continued the stranger. Old Fred beamed, he was not a conceited man, but being praised by this strange little fellow felt good.

"And I know you are a good man," said the stranger.

"You talk to the bees."

"How do you know I talk to my bees?" asked Old Fred. He only talked to the bees when he was alone, and even then, he was mostly talking to himself.

"When you talk to the bees, they listen, Old Fred, and the bees talk to me." Old Fred was intrigued, today had already been a strange one, why shouldn't it get any stranger?

"Who are you?" he asked.

The little man got to his feet and spread his arms as if to present himself. "I am…" he paused. "The Bee Polisher!" And he took a little bow.

"A bee polisher?" Old Fred had never heard of a bee polisher before. "I've never heard of one of those before, what the heck is a bee polisher? You look like a gnome to me."

"Not a bee polisher, The Bee Polisher." Sighed the little man. "There's only one of me, and you need my help, Old Fred."

"How can you help me?" Old Fred asked.

The Bee Polisher sat back down and looked into Old Fred's eyes. Old Fred noticed that in the eyes of The Bee Polisher, there was a youthful twinkle, despite his seemingly ancient, wrinkled face.

"I have been listening to the bees, Old Fred. They are not happy, not happy at all, they are in great danger."

"So I'm told," said Old Fred. "I've heard that the new

Queen is taking them all to the castle. I can't think why."

"She has misunderstood them, and she is hateful and ignorant to the bees and the whole balance of life in the valley. The bees need the flowers and the trees; in the castle, they will surely suffer and die."

"That's terrible!" exclaimed Old Fred. "They can't do that to the bees!"

"It's more than terrible," replied The Bee Polisher. "All the flowers and the crops need the bees too. Without them there will be no crops or flowers. The valley would die and so would everybody left in it."

"But how can you help?" asked Old Fred. "The Queen's soldiers have spears, and you don't look like a warrior or a hero. No offence." He added. "The soldiers are already halfway down the valley. It won't be long before they're here in Coombe after our bees."

"Watch this." Came the reply.

The Bee Polisher turned his gaze towards the beehives. He began to hum, the sound travelling through his bulbous nose, into the air and towards the bees. A bee (one of the stragglers that hadn't yet decided to turn in for the night) stopped it's lazy meandering and made, appropriately, a beeline straight to The Bee Polisher. It came to a stop and hovered inches away from his nose, seemingly waiting for something. The Bee Polisher stopped humming and rummaged beneath his cloak. After some clattering and banging, he produced a jar of what looked like beeswax and a rag.

Old Fred watched on, amazed, as the little chap dipped the rag into the wax and proceeded to rub the wax onto the unprotesting bee.

"They like this they do, Old Fred. Being polished."

The procedure continued, and the bee was getting very shiny indeed. Old Fred didn't know you could polish a bee, he had never thought about doing it himself before and right now, he could not figure out how it could possibly help with their current predicament. Seeming to sense somehow what Old Fred was thinking, The Bee Polisher continued:

"Be patient, Old Fred. You will see…"

The bee was now very, very shiny. It shone in the dusk, twinkling like a star in the night sky.

"By gum!" cried Old Fred. "That's the most beautiful thing I've seen in my whole life!"

"Nearly there now, Old Fred."

"Surely you can't get it any shinier than that?" Old Fred watched, dumbfounded, as the polishing continued. As the polishing continued, he realised he could see the bee less and less until, finally, it vanished.

"Where has it gone? It's disappeared!"

"Don't worry, it's still here, you just can't see it any more. It's see-through."

"See-through? How…"

"Like a window, a clean one. A very, very clean window. Listen…" he whispered.

Old Fred couldn't see the bee any more, but he was aware, if he listened very closely, that he could still hear it buzzing around the orchard, quite happily.

"That's just fantastic!" He said. "The soldiers will never find my bees if they are see-through."

"Precisely," replied the bee polisher. "But there are many bees for me to polish if we are to save your crops, and the soldiers will be here before very long, so I must hurry, I have a lot of work to do."

The next market day in Coombe, Old Fred trundled his cart into the village square, as usual. He spotted Young Bill the butcher's boy staring at a notice pinned onto the usually ignored community noticeboard. Ordinarily, it contained old and forgotten information about the Local Wives and Other Ladies Institute's latest 'Ladies lunch' at the long house on the green. Old Fred could not imagine what, on that noticeboard, could have caught Young Bill's (or anyone else's) attention, and Young Bill couldn't even read. So, he wandered over for a look.

"How do, Young Bill."

"Hello, Old Fred," replied Bill. "There's a new thing

on the board. What's it say, Old Fred? Is there to be a celebration, or a festival? We've not had a single celebration or festival for absolutely ages, well not since the new queen, anyway."

Old Fred read the notice:

WANTED: BEES
To the people of this hamlet

VICIOUS BEES
have been found guilty of an attack
on Her Majesty, your Queen Malicia.
Be warned, for they harbour terrorist ideas.

YOU ARE NOT SAFE!
Please hand over all bees to your
friendly local bee collection officer.

BY ORDER OF THE QUEEN!

This was not good news at all, thought Old Fred.

"What does it say, Old Fred?" asked Young Bill.

"It says the bees are trying to kill the queen, Young Bill."

"Crikey! I'm not surprised the queen's having them all locked up! Who'd have thought it?"

"It says they're terrorists and that we're not safe." Said Old Fred.

"What should we do, Old Fred?"

"Let's not get all carried away with ourselves now, Young Bill."

"But what does it say?" insisted Young Bill.

"It says to hand over all the bees to a friendly local bee collection officer. I wonder who that is?" mused Old Fred.

"Oh no! We've got bees in our garden!" he was clearly distressed. "I must warn my mother!" Young Bill bolted out of the square and raced towards his home.

Old Fred began to unload his cart and set up his market stall. It was a warm day so he positioned the freshest fruit at the front to entice the few locals ambling by. Throughout the morning, he watched folk entering the square, noticing the new notice, and gathering round the noticeboard in small groups, chattering excitedly. The groups would soon disperse and leave quickly, seemingly forgetting all about their shopping plans.

This was disappointing, Old Fred thought as he watched people coming and going again throughout the day. It was harvest time, and Old Fred's produce this year was particularly good. No harvest festival had been announced by the new queen for this year, so there would be no chance for him to display his bumper crop to anybody outside of Coombe.

And what was the big deal with the bees? There had never been a problem with them before, there had always been lots of bees buzzing around the kingdom; they had lived happily alongside bees forever, it seemed. Old Fred had received the odd sting now and again, the worst time being when he had accidentally trod on one with his bare foot, but he was sure it hadn't stung him out of anger or spite.

No, there had to have been some sort of terrible misunderstanding. As far as Old Fred was concerned, bees were mostly friendly. They made delicious honey, and he knew from personal experience that bees also made very good listeners indeed. Many an evening, Old Fred had spent, on his own, just chatting away to his bees; they had always been patient with him, and had never once interrupted him. Sadly, he packed his unsold fruit and vegetables back into his cart, deciding that there was no point hanging around as no one was buying, not wanting his produce to spoil in the heat of the sun.

On the way back to Hunningbie Farm, Old Fred's route took him past Maurice the miller's place. Ordinarily a hive of activity, the mill seemed deserted, its blades, usually turning industriously in the wind, stood motionless against the early evening sky.

As he was trundling past, Old Fred heard a loud shriek of alarm coming from the little cottage beneath the windmill. Old Fred stopped his cart and climbed down, and went to see if he could be of any help. People shrieking in alarm often need some sort of help, he reasoned. He noticed Maurice's old flour cart was not in the yard, which was not unusual as Maurice was often out on his rounds, delivering flour to the bakers in Coombe and other surrounding villages.

Old Fred approached the cottage and knocked on the door.

"Mrs Miller?" he called. Old Fred could hear the sounds of household things being knocked over and broken.

"Mary?" he called again. "Are you alright? It's Old Fred, the farmer! Do you need some help in there?"

Sounds from within indicated someone rushing towards the door. It flew open and out shot a very frightened miller's wife.

"Oh, Old Fred, thank heavens!" she clung to him as if he'd just rescued her from drowning. "I'm so glad it's you! I'm terrified!"

"Whatever's the matter, Mary? Where's Maurice?" asked Old Fred, concerned.

"He's left one!" said Mary. "He's gone up to Mulby with the bees, but he's left one. He said I'd be safe." She sobbed pitifully.

"Left one what?"

Mary pointed a shaking finger towards the cottage door.

"It's in there, look." She whispered, then started sobbing a bit more.

Old Fred, curious, poked his head around the door. The small living room was in gloom because the shutters on the window had been bolted firmly shut. This struck Fred as rather strange. Who would want to block up their windows on such a warm and pleasant day? He stepped cautiously into the room.

Once his eyes had adjusted for the low level of light inside, Old Fred scanned the room. There was nothing there. He scanned the mantlepiece and saw nothing amiss amongst the assorted clutter of ornaments still left on there. A few items had apparently been knocked to the floor in Mary's struggle. There was nothing to be found behind either of the wooden chairs that sat at each end of an old oak table. He looked under the table but again, could see no sign of anything that could be considered alarming.

"Are you sure there's something in here, Mary?" he called. Maybe she's gone mad, he thought.

"Can't you see it?" she called back. "It's definitely in there, it attacked me! I was so scared, I thought I'd never make it out alive!"

No doubt about it, Mary must have indeed gone thoroughly potty, Old Fred thought. It's not really surprising, spending your days grinding flour, bagging flour, loading flour, dusting flour and breathing flour. She never went on the rounds with Maurice, so she probably hasn't seen a proper flower for years.

Feeling some concern for the poor woman, Old Fred made a mental note to have a discreet word with Maurice, and to suggest he maybe treat her to a little holiday or something, to help with his poor wife's nerves, when he could spare the time.

He was about to leave the cottage when he noticed a small bee buzzing around by the window, occasionally bumping gently off the shutters, as if trying to solve some sort of problem. Old Fred watched it for a while, feeling sorry for the little critter. It was trying to get outside, back into the evening sun, back to its hive. He looked around and found a brandy glass and a thin wooden table mat. Carefully, he caught the bee in the glass, then delicately, he slid the table mat between the window shutter and the glass, trapping the bee inside. Old Fred noticed the curve of the glass magnifying the bee, making it look a lot bigger than it actually was. Old Fred made his way back outside.

"There's nothing there, Mary, have you been working yourself too hard? It's no good for you, working too hard."

"I didn't imagine it, Old Fred." Sniffed Mary. "There was def... Aaaargh!" she screamed and pointed at Old Fred. "There it is! Look! You've caught it! It's gigantic! Oh, thank you, Old Fred, you're a hero!"

Old Fred was very confused, then he remembered the bee he had trapped in the glass.

"This? This is what you're so terrified of? It's just a honey bee, Mary. I have lots of them on my farm, there's no cause to worry about the bees. So long as you let them go about their day, they'll let you go about yours. Look."

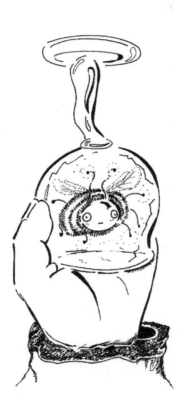

He held out the bee so that Mary could see it better. She yelped and jumped behind some sacks of flour. Old Fred was baffled; how had she lived in the country so long with such a severe and irrational phobia?

"Don't worry, Mary, I'll take it over here and let it go. It shouldn't bother you again." Old Fred started to walk towards the lane.

"Let it go?" Mary sounded shocked. "Let it go? You can't just let it loose again. They're dangerous, Old Fred, haven't you heard? They're wanted for terrorist crimes. You have to take it to the friendly local bee collection officer; that's where Maurice is now, in Mulby, handing in all our bees, all except this one, anyway."

"Come on now, Mary," said Old Fred. "Maurice isn't a fool, he wouldn't hand all his bees, all except this one, over to somebody he doesn't know, for no good reason at all."

"You're right, Old Fred," she replied. "Maurice is not a fool, that's why he's handing them in. It's the law, and you should go over to Mulby right now and hand over that bee and all the bees you have down there on your farm, otherwise you could get into a lot of trouble!"

"I'll take the bee, Mary." Old Fred was already troubled, this bee was not a threat to anybody, least of all the Queen. He placed the glass and table mat down on the ground and fished around in his pockets, eventually pulling out a box of matches. He emptied the contents into his pocket then, very carefully, removed the bee from its little glass prison and transferred it into the matchbox.

"I'll be on my way now, Mary, I hope you'll be feeling a bit better before too long."

"Thank you, Old Fred, you saved me from that menace, I'm sure I'll be all recovered soon."

"Think nothing of it. Give Maurice my regards when he gets back."

"I will," said Mary. "And thank you again."

Old Fred climbed up into his cart, more than ready to be back on the farm. It seemed to be the only sane place left in the world, even if it did currently have The Bee Polisher working away there, with his beeswax and rag. As he started down the lane, he heard Mary call after him.

"Don't forget to hand in your bees!"

Old Fred sighed.

The Royal Twill buzzed with activity. Literally buzzed. Queen Malicia was feeling very pleased with herself, the dungeons were filling up nicely now that most of the people were actually catching their own bees and handing them in without even questioning why. The friendly local bee collection officers had been a stroke of genius, they were trusted because they were both friendly and local.

Manipulating other people is easy when you are a queen, she thought to herself, smugly.

The guards were now free to spend their resources on 'encouraging' the less willing among the people, those who would not hand over their bees just because they had been told to do so. The encouragement usually came in the form of a stern talking to, but it could occasionally stretch to the smashing up of possessions and the not-so-hidden threat to harm family and friends. These methods seemed to work very effectively, and they had already managed to clear nearly the whole kingdom of the rotten little bees. There was a knock on the throne room door; Malicia had been expecting it.

"You may enter, Captain!" she called.

The door creaked open and the Captain of the Guard entered, removing his helmet as he did so. He tucked it neatly under his left arm and made an appropriately respectful bow to the queen.

"Your Majesty, I am here to give you my report on the progress of the operation so far."

"Thank you, Captain, you may deliver your report. I trust the news is all good? I trust things are moving smoothly? No major problems?"

Somewhere inside her voice, there was a tiny hint of menace, very tiny but very obviously there, and very obviously menacing. The captain decided not to worry the queen with rumours of a few villagers smuggling bees into the kingdom to replace the ones that had been taken from them. There really were just a few, so it would probably be for the best not to mention it for the time being.

"No problems, Your Majesty," replied the captain, in a courageous act of self-preservation. "The troops only have a few small towns and villages to process, then the war on this terror shall be won. Congratulations, Your Majesty."

"Let's not pat ourselves on the back just yet, Captain. We need to get rid of all traces of these devil bees forever, if the people do not see us vanquish all enemies, how could they have any respect for me as their ruler? We must be absolutely and convincingly triumphant. Complacency could make us a laughing stock both here in the Kingdom and amongst all the other kings and queens around the world."

"Very true, Your Majesty." Said the captain. "You are very wise indeed, my Queen."

"Tell your men to redouble their efforts and leave no stone unturned. There can be no victory celebrations until we know for certain that there is not a single bee left in this Kingdom. Not one."

"As you wish, Your Majesty."

The captain bowed and marched out of the room. As the door closed behind him, Queen Malicia turned to the balcony and surveyed her kingdom. She could just imagine the adoration of her people when she, their queen, had saved them from the peril of the bees.

"Malicia," she said aloud to herself, "you are a genius."

The Queen grinned.

In the orchard at Hunningbie Farm, The Bee Polisher had been busy as a creature that, when observed, could be imagined to be very busy indeed. He turned to Old Fred as he had wandered into the orchard after his bizarre day at the market, and the even more bizarre goings on at the mill.

"Hello, Old Fred, my friend. I have almost finished polishing your bees, I fear we might not have long left before the Queen's soldiers will be here to try to take your bees."

"Probably sooner than you think," sighed Old Fred. "Everyone's just giving their bees up. I don't understand, do people actually believe the bees are evil and dangerous?"

"People are easy to fool when they are scared," replied The Bee Polisher, sadly. "The Queen has cast a spell of fear across the kingdom she has sworn to protect, and the people are afraid. She has told them the bees are evil, and filled their heads with untruths, and they believe her."

"But don't they remember that before the notices went up, they weren't afraid of the bees? We've lived with the bees forever."

"Memories of the past are short and soon forgotten when fear of the future is present."

"Well, I've had bees all my life and I've never seen one doing anything bad, or even a little bit naughty. Bees are possibly some of the nicest and most useful creatures about, in my humble opinion."

Old Fred sat down beneath the apple tree, he was extremely tired, concerned and confused about everything that had been going on.

"I believe you to be correct, Old Fred." The Bee Polisher put down his rag, the bee he was currently polishing hovered patiently, shining beautifully in the dwindling evening light. "They dance too."

"I've seen them dancing to each other," said Old Fred.

"Ah, the waggle dance." Sighed The Bee Polisher, misty eyed with the romance of the thought.

"Why do they dance? Who teaches them?" asked Old Fred.

"They dance to show each other the way of the bees. Nobody knows how they know to dance." The Bee Polisher answered. "I believe it's ancient bee magic."

"Ancient bee magic?" Old Fred had never heard of ancient bee magic before. "I've never heard of ancient bee magic before."

"It's only my opinion, but I believe they must have magic. How else could you explain the wonder of honey?"

Old Fred contemplated this for a while and decided he could not find fault with the little chap's logic. It seemed to make complete sense to him.

Old Fred rested back on the tree trunk and watched as The Bee Polisher carried on with his work, diligently and industriously polishing away, bee after bee being shined into invisibility. It was hypnotic.

"Last one now, Old Fred."

Fred awoke with a start. He must have dozed off while watching The Bee Polisher.

"I didn't like to wake you, Old Fred, but I thought you might like to see the completion of my work."

Old Fred yawned and mumbled something that could possibly have meant The Bee Polisher was not wrong. The final bee buzzed towards them, it was much bigger than the rest.

"The Queen," said The Bee Polisher dreamily.

The Bee Polisher gazed at the queen bee and bowed out of respect. Old Fred found himself bowing too.

"Hello, Your Majesty," said The Bee Polisher softly. "It's a pleasure to meet you."

The Queen seemed to bob in the air, as if accepting The Bee Polisher into her presence. Old Fred looked on, awestruck.

"May I introduce my friend, Old Fred, Ma'am?"

The Queen bee seemed to bob again, this time in Old Fred's direction. "She likes you, Old Fred."

"Erm..." Old Fred gulped. The Bee Polisher chuckled.

"Oh, Old Fred!" He laughed. "You've spent your whole life chatting away to the bees, not knowing if they were even listening. Now you meet the Queen and you're lost for words!" The Bee Polisher gave Old Fred a friendly wink.

"Er, hello, Your Majesty?" attempted Old Fred, weakly. The Bee Polisher chuckled and the queen bee did a little loop-the-loop, as if she was also in on the joke.

"Don't fret, Old Fred," said The Bee Polisher. "It's not every day you get to meet a queen."

Old Fred began to chuckle, he could see the funny side. He looked at The Bee Polisher, who was still chuckling away. Old Fred's chuckle became a laugh and soon the pair of them were clutching their stomachs in hysterics, the queen bee dancing around them. Old Fred hadn't laughed so hard in years, not since the village drunk, Dennis, had lost his bet that he could jump clean over Old Fred's manure pile.

Eventually, they calmed down enough to catch their breath. Old Fred was exhausted and his ribs were hurting, but he was happy. The queen bee was back in front of The Bee Polisher, who was ready and waiting with his rag and polish. He began slowly and carefully to polish her, whispering to her as he did so.

"Now, Your Majesty, Old Fred here's your friend. He's going to keep you safe and hidden from the soldiers."

He carried on whispering to her as he worked. The queen bee hummed contentedly. Soon she began to shine, and before long she was glowing, glowing, gone.

"It is finished." Said The Bee Polisher. He picked up his jar of polish and put it, along with his rag, back somewhere inside his cloak.

"Well, Old Fred, my work here is done." He turned to leave.

"Surely you don't have to leave straight away!" cried Old Fred. "You could stay for a while! What about the bees? What about the soldiers?"

The Bee Polisher looked back at Old Fred, and smiled.

"Do not worry, Old Fred. Your bees are see-through now, the soldiers will not be able to find them and they have you to protect them, my friend. Just remember, when the bees talk, I listen."

Old Fred watched the strange little form of The Bee

Polisher as he made his way towards the beehives. Eventually he disappeared into the gloom. Old Fred was sad, he liked the little chap, he may have been a bit strange, but he seemed to have made more sense than anybody else he had spoken to recently. He sat for a while longer, gazing at the beehives, then, realising how tired he was, Old Fred got to his feet and made his way inside his cottage for a well-earned sleep.

BANG, BANG, BANG!

"Open up in the name of the Queen!"

Old Fred woke up, not in the name of the Queen, but because some maniac was banging loudly on his door. Who could this possibly be at this time in the morning?

BANG, BANG, BANG!

"Open up in the name of the Queen!"

Old Fred sat up. It didn't sound like the Queen. He had never heard the Queen speak before, but whoever was shouting did not sound like a queen, this was definitely a man's voice. He put on his dressing down.

BANG, BANG, BANG!

"Open up in the name of..."

"...the Queen?" Fred yawned.

The man at the door was short and thin. The only way

Fred could describe him would have to be pointy. His face was pointy. He had a pointy nose, pointy chin, pointy ears, pointy eyebrows - even his hat was pointy. On his dark blue hat was emblazoned the letters F.L.B.C.O. in gold letters.

"What's all this about? It's first thing in the morning! Who are you?" Old Fred yawned again and rubbed his eyes.

"I am your friendly local bee collection officer." The pointy man pointed towards the lettering on his hat. "I am here to collect your bees. By order of the Queen!"

"Local? I don't know you, I've never seen you before. You're not from round here."

"Well, I am here, on your doorstep. What can be more local than your own front door? I am locally collecting your bees in a friendly manner. By order of the Queen!" He shouted 'the Queen!' almost loud enough that the Queen herself might possibly have heard it from the castle.

"Well in that case, I'm afraid you've had a wasted journey," said Old Fred, stretching some life into his newly woken arms. "All of my bees have disappeared, you'll find no bees here."

"Then you won't mind if my associates and I take a look around, if you have nothing to hide." The friendly local bee collection officer motioned to his associates. His associates were three very large soldiers dressed in full armour.

"See for yourself, I'll show you the beehives, you'll see no bees." Old Fred, still in his dressing gown and slippers, led the friendly local bee collection officer, and his associates, towards the orchard.

"Moo."

"Good morning, Milky Joe," called Old Fred as they

passed the barn.

"Moo."

"Don't worry, Milky Joe, these good people are just passing through. They won't be long, then we'll get you out in the field."

"Moo." Milky Joe eyed the group suspiciously as they passed.

Old Fred led the friendly local bee collection officer and his heavily armed escorts through the orchard towards the beehives. The friendly local bee collection officer inspected them closely; he saw nothing.

"Like I told you," said Old Fred. "You won't see any bees around here, they have disappeared."

"What's that buzzing noise I can hear then? Explain that."

"Er, tinnitus?" Old Fred ventured. "You should get your ears checked." The friendly local bee collection officer did not appear the slightest bit amused.

"Not voluntarily handing over your bees upon demand is a serious and punishable criminal offence." The friendly local bee collection officer turned to his guards.

"Search this whole farm, thoroughly!" He commanded.

"By order of the Queen?" asked Old Fred cheekily.

"Yes. By order of the Queen!" added the friendly local bee collection officer.

The soldiers began their search, their method of searching seemed to be to knock things over, and to occasionally stab their spears into random shrubs and hay piles. Old Fred watched as they turned his farm upside down; chickens, geese and ducks flew everywhere as they scoured the farmyard. Milky Joe was not happy at all when they attempted to search the barn. Old Fred heard the commotion and entered the barn to see the soldiers surrounding his prize cow, pointing their spears menacingly at her.

"Come with me, Milky Joe." He led the cow out of the barn and let her into the field. Returning to the farmyard, Old Fred spoke to the friendly local bee collection officer.

"You'll find nothing here, as I said, they've disappeared."

"We shall see." Came the reply.

"Well, if you don't mind, I'd like to get some proper clothes on." Old Fred didn't like wearing his slippers outside, it wore them out.

"Of course, you must get dressed," the friendly local bee collection officer said, benevolently. "Guard!" A soldier approached. "Watch him closely."

Old Fred walked through the cottage to his bedroom and got dressed, under the watchful eye of the guard. He strolled back towards the friendly local bee collection officer. The soldiers continued their search, generally upturning the furniture and throwing things around. After a while, they finished and came outside.

"There's nothing here, sir."

The friendly local bee collection officer frowned and turned to Fred.

"It seems this is indeed a bee free zone. I am sorry to have inconvenienced you."

Old Fred took out his pipe.

"It'll take me all day to clean this mess up. Local? Friendly? I don't think so."

He pulled a matchbox out of his pocket. As he opened it, the bee Old Fred had rescued from the mill the day before flew out, bounced off the friendly local bee collection officer's nose, and buzzed away.

"Guards!" screamed the friendly local bee collection officer. "Arrest this man, and catch that bee. By order of the Queen!"

Old Fred had visited The Royal Twill many years before. He had been personally invited to the kingdom's capital, Bumbleton, by King Garold himself, as a reward for the quality of the fruit he had produced. It had been a happy and memorable occasion; as a hard-working farmer, it was very rare to be able to travel anywhere for leisure, and Fred had thoroughly enjoyed the experience.

This time, as Fred was escorted by soldiers into the castle, personally invited, not voluntarily, by Queen Malicia, was very different. The pointy, friendly local bee collection officer bowed low.

"Your Majesty, we have brought you the last bee in the kingdom!" he produced the matchbox. "We have also brought you the villain that has been harbouring the terrorist threat. Guards!"

The soldiers presented Old Fred, in shackles, to the Queen. She eyed the old farmer with distaste.

"So, you are a traitor, and an enemy of the throne. You have allowed terrorist bees space and sanctuary in which to hatch their evil plots against me. We shall make an example of you. There will be no doubt what happens to traitors in my kingdom."

"It was just a bee," replied Old Fred. "It was trapped so I helped it. It wasn't hurting anybody."

"Silence!" screamed Queen Malicia. "Take him to the dungeons and lock him up while we decide his fate!"

Old Fred was led away, by order of the Queen. The soldiers took him down what seemed like hundreds and hundreds of stairs, all the while the humming from all the captured bees grew louder as they got closer to the dungeons. In the throne room, Malicia consulted with the Captain of the Guard.

"We shall chop off his head! That will show the people what becomes of treachery in this land!" shouted Queen Malicia.

"Er, there's no death penalty in Bumblonia, Your Majesty," replied the captain. "They have never had a traitor before."

"Then we shall keep him locked up until we can sort it out, how hard can it be?"

What was the point of being a queen if you can't chop people's heads off when you wanted to, thought Malicia.

The winter had been a typically cold one. A sheet of snow had lain, as usual, over Bumblonia before, eventually, melting into the valley floor. Not in a position to appreciate this changing of the seasons, Old Fred's spirits were low. The dungeons were not particularly comfortable, and offered no view to the outside world. He had run out of things to talk to the bees about, and their near constant buzzing seemed to be getting louder and more impatient with the arrival of spring.

All through the kingdom, the people had been waiting for the land to wake up, and they were still waiting. The bright colours of the wild flowers seemed not to be quite as bright or widespread as they usually were. The vegetable crops were also poor and across the kingdom, a definite atmosphere of worry prevailed.

Queen Malicia was aware of the troubled feelings that abounded in Bumblonia, and had brought in some 'experts' to try to solve the problem. The 'experts' had travelled the length and breadth of the land and had discovered a strange anomaly. They had found that one farm at the bottom of the valley, near the village of Coombe, seemed to be abundant with wild flowers, and its orchard was blooming healthily. There was no sign of the farmer so they reported their findings back to the queen.

"Hunningbie Farm?" mused Malicia, aloud. "Why does that sound familiar to me?"

"We apprehended the last bee in the kingdom on

Hunningbie Farm, Your Majesty," answered the captain. "I believe we still have the miscreant farmer that was hiding it in custody here at the castle."

"Have we not chopped off his head yet? Bring him to me at once!" ordered the Queen.

Old Fred was soon standing, in his shackles, before Queen Malicia. He did not particularly want to be standing, in shackles, before Queen Malicia, but at least it was a change from the cold and uncomfortable dungeons that had been his home for the past few months. The Queen paced up close to Fred and stared into his eyes.

"It seems there is yet another curse on my Kingdom," she snarled. "I have got rid of the devil bees that were threatening the realm, yet the crops are failing. There soon shan't be enough food and the people will starve."

"That's not good news, Your Majesty." Mumbled Old Fred.

"The crops are failing everywhere except on one farm, yours," said Malicia, accusingly. "Explain yourself."

"I don't know what to say, Your Majesty," said Fred, not knowing what to say. "I've been here in the castle all winter, I can't account for the crops failing."

"I can't account for the crops failing," mimicked the Queen cruelly. "Then account for your crops not failing." She hissed in Old Fred's face.

"All I can say is that I am pleased Hunningbie Farm sounds to be doing well without me," Old Fred was pleased; he had missed his farm, especially Milky Joe. "It must be the bees."

"Bees, what bees?" screamed the Queen. "There are no bees left free in the kingdom. Not one! We captured the last one along with you."

Old Fred reasoned that he probably couldn't get into any more trouble than he already was in, so he continued.

"My bees are still on the farm, they are see-through, you see?"

"See-through?" the Queen didn't understand. "What on earth do you mean, see-through? I don't understand!"

"It was The Bee Polisher." Old Fred announced, proudly.

"A bee polisher? A bee polisher? There's no such thing!" the Queen fumed.

"Not a bee polisher," sighed a voice from the back of the room. "The Bee Polisher."

The little cloaked figure couldn't be more than a foot tall. He had seemed to appear from nowhere, and was immediately surrounded by a rather confused looking bunch of guards. They collectively pointed their spears, menacingly, in the direction of The Bee Polisher. None of them had ever seen such a little fellow as this before. Old

Fred was delighted to see his little friend again, although admittedly, it would have been a much nicer reunion had it been in different surroundings, but it was good to see him anyway.

"What the devil are you, gnome?" Queen Malicia hissed.

"I am not a gnome, thank you very much, I am The Bee Polisher, and I have made Old Fred here's bees see-through. You were sworn to protect all life in the kingdom and you have not. Your bitterness and ignorance has led to you putting the lives of everybody in the land at risk."

"How dare you?" the Queen's face had turned a colour of deep red in her rage. "How dare you speak to your Queen in such a manner? I'll chop off your head!"

"I think not," The Bee Polisher spoke calmly. "I believe there is somebody you should meet."

The throne room door swung open and a strange man danced in. The guards turned, unsure who they should be guarding against: Old Fred, the newly arrived stranger, or The Bee Polisher. The stranger danced right up close to the furious looking Queen.

"So you must be the nasty new Queen that I've heard so many terrible things about." He sang.

Queen Malicia's face turned an even brighter shade of red with her growing rage.

"Who do you think you are?" she screamed. "Guards! Arrest this man at once!"

The guards pointed their spears towards the dancing stranger.

"My name is Barold, son of old King Garold," laughed Barold, son of old King Garold. "I have been learning the ancient dances of the creatures in the kingdom, including the waggle dance."

"The waggle dance?" mocked the Queen. "What's the

waggle dance?"

"The waggle dance is the dance of the bees," answered Barold. "It is an ancient dance used by the bees to show them the way. Without it, the crops and plants of the kingdom cannot reproduce, which would be a complete disaster, the people would starve."

Old Fred looked on as Barold danced round the angry Queen. It seemed to him that he was, thankfully, no longer the focus of anyone's attention. The Bee Polisher appeared to have disappeared again as well.

"You have failed the people of the kingdom and all the life therein," continued Barold. "They need a ruler that understands the things that are important so I am here to reclaim my rightful throne, my birthright!"

"Clap him in irons!" ordered Malicia.

The guards surrounded Barold menacingly. As they did so, a buzzing from the direction of the dungeons was gradually growing louder. A door in a side wall flew open and there stood The Bee Polisher. He entered the throne room followed by all the bees that had been held captive by the Queen. They flew in and swarmed round the queen and her guards who immediately fled, screaming, from the castle. The bees gave chase and soon Malicia and her guards were seen, screaming, and racing right out of the Kingdom, in the general direction of Shmogg.

A month had passed since the now famous incident at The Royal Twill. Barold was crowned with a simple wreath, in a simple ceremony at which Old Fred and The Bee Polisher had been honoured guests.

It had been a month of celebrations throughout the land; the folk were pleased to have seen the back of Queen Malicia and her guards.

Old Fred was overjoyed to be back on Hunningbie Farm. He had politely and humbly declined King Barold's invitation to stay at the castle. He missed his home, especially Milky Joe. The Bee Polisher agreed to stay a little longer to act as Royal Advisor of all things to do with bees. The first thing King Barold did was to issue an official royal pardon to all the bees in the Kingdom of Bumblonia.

Old Fred sat in the orchard, smoking his pipe, not watching his bees, as they were still see-through. As the smoke from his pipe drifted gently towards the beehives, Old Fred noticed a cloaked figure that seemed to have appeared from out of nowhere.

The first thing Old Fred noticed was the height of the fellow, he couldn't be more than a foot tall, which was rather short for people in these parts. The strange little man approached and as he got nearer to Old Fred, he could see he looked very old. He walked with a stick, although he did not seem to have a limp and did not seem to be very frail. Old Fred noticed that the bees had started humming in their hives.

"Hello there," said Old Fred, unsurprised. Nothing surprised Old Fred any more, not after the things he had seen recently.

"Hello, Old Fred," said the strange little man.

Yet again, Old Fred was unsurprised. Everyone in the kingdom knew Old Fred's name now; he was quite the celebrity, having been instrumental in the ridding of the nasty old Queen Malicia.

The strange little man approached Old Fred and sat down. Old Fred noticed that in the eyes of the fellow, there was a youthful twinkle, despite his seemingly ancient, wrinkled face.

The stranger pulled a tiny brush from under his cloak, and a tin of what appeared to be yellow and black striped paint. He turned to Old Fred.

"It is good to finally meet you, Old Fred, I have heard a lot about you. I believe you know my cousin," said the little chap, dipping his brush into the paint.

"Allow me to introduce myself. I am... The Bee Painter!"

The End